HAZEL EYES
A FABLE

Marvin Patton

and

Carol Gerrior-Patton

ISBN: 13: 978-0692150184
ISBN: 10: 0692150188

Marvin L. Patton and Carol J. Gerrior-Patton

HAZELWOOD TREE

HAZELNUT OR FILBERT

Marvin L. Patton and Carol J. Gerrior-Patton

SPECIAL THANKS

We want to thank the following friends
and professionals for helping, advising,
and encouraging, organizing, and
gracefully critiquing us throughout the
work on our books:
Ryan Cole: Technical Support genius;
Rudolph C. Schafer: Business advisor
Almut McCauley: Writing professor
Jack Valenti: President of the MPAA
Bud Boetticher: Film Director, Mentor
Larry Huffman: Announcer, Producer
James A. Michener: A fan and supporter

DEDICATION

To children of all ages
From childhood to childhood
A rich imagination dresses the
mind
From our youth
And gives grace in our older years.

OTTER

COLOR ME!

Marvin L. Patton and Carol J. Gerrior-Patton

BEAVER

COLOR ME!

CONTENT

Page 1: Hazel Eyes

Marvin L. Patton and Carol J. Gerrior-Patton

OWL

COLOR ME!

Hazel Eyes – A Fable

Marvin L. Patton and Carol J. Gerrior-Patton

COLOR ME!
RAVEN!

COLOR ME!
CROW!

ACKNOWLEDGMENTS

To our Creator who gave us our
imagination.
To our teachers and fellow students at
show and tell time;
To our parents who read the notes our
teachers sent home with us afterwards.
To all the corners we had to sit in and
the dunce hats we had to wear...
To the principals that tried to teach us
their principles through the paddle...
To the fireflies who shine in flight; to
the poet who gives the sentence might...
To all those who read this story and
find delight.

Thank you!

Marvin L. Patton and Carol J. Gerrior-Patton

Hazel Eyes
A Fable

Once, when the virgin forest and country of the far north only knew the ways of nature and not of mankind, fertile seeds of a new species of the birch family—the Hazelwood—were planted by Creator and began to grow throughout the region. One of the young seedlings, near the foot of a fan-shaped meadow, inundated with a sea of attractive and colorful wild flowers, and blending in with stands of birch, white pine, oaks, willows, and hundreds upon hundreds of thick towering firs and spruces that spread out in all directions from the lovely meadow, was well into its fourth year of growth. To the south, west and the east of the young sapling were beaver ponds of various sizes. The shore line was overwhelmed with towering Tule reeds, marsh grasses, and lily pads. And there were various beaver homes of all shapes and sizes spread out in the middle of the ponds. And just beyond the meadow and ponds were pristine lakes that had been created during the ice age. A crystal clear stream flowed nearby, and as it meandered its way south to a much larger body of water, it gave the forest a delightful and continuous

1

rippling harmony as it flowed over the rocks and stones of various sizes and colors. Throughout the evening hours, and well into the nights, came the sound of crickets and other insects—along with the cries of ducks and loons from off the large lake that extended over the southern horizon.

The light brown sapling, with a tinge of green and gold, was the latest deciduous tree created; a special tree that man would eventually call the Ha-zelnut. It was one of the first of thousands created and planted within the northern sector of the virgin forest, and while all the others were thriving rather well, this one in particular, with its contrasting splendor, was planted to enhance the nearby meadow with its tooth like leaves, its yellow and greenish-brown branches and stems, and more than anything else, it was to be a precious gift to help sustain life with its egg-shaped edible filberts, and its grandeur was to delight and draw all that passed it by to observe its enchanting flowers and to sample its delicious fruit.

But something was terribly wrong.

It was in its fourth year of growth and it had become sickly. Creator was concerned. Its branches, stems, and young leaves were beginning to droop down-ward. Creator knew the young tree was going to expire if something wasn't done. It's true that Creator could heal the young bush with just speaking it to be healthy, but He had faith in all His creations and knew the animals living in the area would all work together to aid in helping to heal His creation. So He whispered a plea to the Gentle Breeze that carried His message over the rugged mountains and through the valleys and across the lovely meadows and pristine lakes and meandering streams.

The first to sense Creator's call for help were two quick and agile Otters. They had been mates for a little over a season and had come to call each other by their own chosen names. The male Otter picked Tanu, which meant industrious and capable; and the female Otter, after careful consideration, decided to go with Elly, a celestial name meaning one who is close to the Creator. The two Otters were well known for their understanding of their surroundings, and the connection that their presence meant to all the other creatures that inhabited the virgin forest.

So it was no wonder to the small, highly vocal and brightly colored finches and warblers, and the dull brown and gray wrens and swallows, and the other avian songsters: the robins and the bluebirds who lived high above them in the nearby trees to see the two playful Otters, who had been sliding down a steep bank and into the nearby stream, to scurry through the underbrush and through the deep green grass of the meadow to the young sapling. Upon their arrival the two Otters sniffed at the young tree's base, its sickly looking leaves, and its drooping branches gave both of them an overpowering feeling in the pit of their stomachs.

"This must be the new tree that Creator is concerned about?" Elly said after sniffing at the base again. Her countenance saddened and tears began to fill her warm, dark eyes.

"It is," Tanu replied.

"I remember it from last year with all its beautiful colorsand edible nuts. Do you?"

"I do," Tanu said with a concern of his own. "Its lovely flowers had such a wonderful scent. And its leaves were exquisite."

"Do you smell or see any diseases?" Elly asked. "I don't." She moved in close to the young tree and began to examine its leaves more closely.

"Nor do I," Tanu said with a hint of sadness. "Nor any signs of fungus."

"Perhaps it has a virus," Elly said in the form of a question?"

"I don't think so," Tanu said after sitting on

his hind legs. He scratched his head, just behind his right ear. "And so far no caterpillars have attached themselves to the young tree." He continued to scratch his head in dismay. "I wonder if it's being fed too much water."

"Root drowning?" Elly asked with a puzzled look.

"Maybe," Tanu said, slowly shaking his head from side-to-side. "I just don't know? The grass and the dirt are dry."

Elly moved over and sat down next to Tanu. "What can we do?" She asked her face still troubled with thoughtful concern in her dark eyes. Tanu did not respond. He just sat on his hind legs shaking his head from side-to-side.

They stared at the young tree and with each passing second they both became more and more inclined to help and to support the change that Creator so desperately needed to save one of His new creations. They sniffed at the tree again and then walked slowly around it. The wind was picking up and they stopped to listen to the rustling leaves of the oak and birch trees. And the soothing motion of the pine needles on the large evergreens that stood tall and proud alongside the winding course of the stream that began its descent above the tall and rolling mountain peaks, near the base of the great white sheet of thick ice.

Creator, in His loving and mysterious ways, was speaking to the two clever and helpful Otters. He was grateful that they had come to help and knew they were deeply troubled. So with the help of Gentle Breeze and the green leaves and pointed needles of the towering pines, He enlightened them on what to do. When the music of the leaves and pine needles stopped, and Gentle Breeze had moved upward to sooth the tops of the branches of the evergreens, the two silky Otters began to dig holes near the base of the young tree, at each compass point. High above them, the songbirds, with their elaborate and various repertoires, fluttered from tree to tree, filling the virgin forest with their chippering throaty songs. They watched the two Otters with curiosity, sending their messages of hope and faith from species to species. Within a few minutes all the lovely birds knew that help had arrived and they may still be able to enjoy another season of the tree's wonderful tasting nuts. Soon all the nearby trees' branches and stems had hundreds of colorful finches and warblers watching the Otters below them.

"What do you think we are digging for?"

Elly asked, "Termites or beetles?"

"I'm not sure," Tanu replied, as he stopped digging for a moment to sniff the air. "But I hope it's not worms or insects." Tanu paused and sighed deeply, rubbing his nose. "But if we do come across a den of worms or bugs, the birds above us will have a feast. That's for sure."

"I agree." Elly said, then stood on her hind legs and sniffed the air. "Beaver is coming." She said, knowingTanu had sensed him first.

"I'm not surprised," Tanu said, looking over his right shoulder to see Beaver emerge from the undergrowth and wobble toward them. "He likes to help."

Beaver was the engineer of the animal kingdom who had an innate passion to dam creeks and streams. He was indeed the second creature to arrive and lend a hand, as he was a consistent, steadfast, and dependable amphibious rodent with dense waterproof brown fur, large chestnut-colored incisors and webbed hind feet and a flat tale. Beaver loved to help strengthen roots, plants, and trees, usually during the night, the early morn-ings, or just before dusk. Beaver began to dig right beside the Otters without comment, as he, too, having heard the plea through gentle breeze on this lovely spring afternoon. He, too, knew this sapling was special and would change the environment for a haven and beauty. It had to be saved and he was determined to do whatever it took to save it.

He spoke after they had finished digging three holes.

"Well there are no insects around this young tree that could surely kill it within a short period of time." Beaver ran his tongue across his two large incisors. "Do you have any idea as to why we are digging these holes?"

"I'm not sure," Tanu replied, "but Creator wants it done. That is the message I heard from gentle breeze in the whispering leaves."

"That is what I heard as well," Elly said, as she began to dig the fourth hole.

"So far there's been no sign of root drowning," Beaver said, as he moved over to help Elly dig the fourth and final hole.

"So we noticed." Elly said, pawing at the ground. "That's good!"

"If we save this tree," Beaver said, as he continued to dig, "it's going to bring a lot of beauty to this place. Look at those old oaks and birch trees near the stream. They are nearing the end of their lives□ much too soon."

"How can you tell?" Elly asked, curiosity

sparkling in her soft eyes.

"The caterpillars of the gypsy moth have been devouring the foliage of the oaks and the birches for weeks. Look at all the songbirds that come to feed on the caterpillars. Every day they come and root out quite a few, but there are so many. I give the trees one more season, if that, and then they will be destroyed."

"Are you sure?"

"Yes," Beaver said sadly. "I have seen it too many times."

A large shadow passed over them and the three friends looked up into the blue sky and observed Owl circling overhead. They all shuddered uncontrollably at the sight of the large flesh eating avis.

"I wonder why she's here in broad daylight," Elly asked, after swallowing the lump of fear in her throat.

"She's come to help us," Beaver said as he continued to watch the large bird circling above them. "She is letting herself be seen so we won't have to fear for our lives."

"It must be The Wise-One," Tanu piped in. "She's a friend. But I wonder where her sister, Gog, is? I haven't seen her in weeks?"

"Well, if it is The Wise-One, we have nothing to worry about," Elly said, then went back to work on the fourth hole.

The others followed her lead.

The Wise-One was the third one to arrive to help. The enduringOwl, the bird of wisdom circled quietly and effortlessly for a few more minutes and then softly landed near the three hard workers when they were finished with the fourth and final hole. The afternoon was turning warm and Beaver began cleaning his body to stay cool. The Owl, the Wise-One, had a soft and controlled glowing fire within her heart; a fire that continually sought and acquired knowledge to understand the changing world. One of her daily routines, just after arising to hunt the creatures of the night, was to sit perched just out-side her den and listen to the wisdom that Creator spread through the whispering pines. She, in turn, would share her new knowledge with all her friends.

"As you know," she said learnedly to get their attention, "I am known for my insight and my convictions. I am pleased to see that you are just as adventurous and excited about life and transforming the world." She hobbled over to the tree and examined the four holes. "You have done a good job. Your hard work is indeed a good sign and Creator will be pleased."

Elly moved a little closer to the Owl and asked: "Where's your sister? We have not seen Gog for weeks? Is she sick?"

"No, she claims that Creator wanted her to leave her territory for a few months and fly out west to seek new knowledge. She's been gone for over two full moons. She will return."

"I hope you're right," Elly said."

"I am," The Owl replied. "Creator has assured me that she is well."

Tanu stood on his hind legs and sniffed, then asked: "Have you come to help this sapling or have you come to just chatter away at the breeze?"

"Tanu," Elly said, "please; don't be so rude."

Tanu glanced at Elly and started to respond but the look in his mate's eyes stopped him. He looked over at The Wise-One. "Sorry," he said shamefaced, watching Elly from the corner of his eyes for approval. "I didn't mean to be so harsh."

The Owl grinned at Tanu. "No harm my friend. It's okay."

"Thank you," Tanu replied and then sighed deeply. "We're a bit on edge, not understanding what and why the young sapling is sickly."

"You're not alone. Look at all the birds in the trees. They, and all the others who live in the region, are concerned too. They love the taste of the nuts and they love the smell of the trees blossoms. As much as we all do."

The two Otters and Beaver looked up at all the lovely birds sitting on the branches and the stems, fluttering their wings and warbling the trills of their throaty songs.

"We must do more," Beaver said, "Any suggestions 'Old Wise One?'"

"You, of all creatures, should know that Owls do not partake in the same rigorous tasks as you. But I have taken everything into consideration and can say without equivocation that you three have done a splendid job. And I also see that you have not disturbed this young tree's roots. That is good. However, you have overlooked one impediment. "

"Really," said Beaver, also sitting up on its hind legs and flat tail. "And just what is that?"

"There's too much shade. Far too much for this young sapling to survive. Take a look at that stand of trees near the stream. They must be thinned out. There's too much shade coming from them. Perhaps one of the large oaks should come down?"

"I thought you and your sister lived in the

oak trees?" Tanu asked.

"We did but we moved to the large spruce shortly after the white hooded Eagles left the area. We occupy it now."

"We were just discussing those trees," Elly chimed in. "Beaver says the trees are being devoured by caterpillars."

"He's right about that," The Wise-One said, nodding her head up and down.

"Gypsy moths invaded the area shortly after the snow melted to lay their eggs," Beaver said. "Their offspring are indeed destroying them." He paused to look at the two oaks. "We should take them down soon. That will provide enough light for the young new sapling and cross pollinators growing just beyond the stream. The remaining trees will give them just the right amount of shade and protection from the cold and wind.

Tanu exchanged glances with Beaver and then moved over to where Elly and The Wise-One stood and observed the sun starved sapling.

"I suggest," Owl went on, looking over at Beaver, "that you call upon your dependable and hard-working brothers and sisters and cousins to begin in haste to chew down the big oak in the center, and perhaps some others to thin out the area. It will also help this young tree to regain its ability to survive by receiving more sunlight throughout the remaining days of the warm period."

"It will need its strength," Tanu added. "We have had three gentle seasons but my instincts are telling me that this coming period of cold days will be long, hard and bitter on all of us."

"If what you say is true," The Wise-One said, eyeing the tall oaks and the birch trees near the stream, "as I said before we must work quickly to save this sapling. Those oaks and birch trees must come down quickly to allow—"

"We'll get them down," Beaver said assuringly, cutting The Wise-One off. "We had a meeting two days ago and we all decided to work in teams and chew them down. The first shift starts tonight. Give us about three days. The task shall be carried out and it will be a thorough job." Beaver paused and proudly grinned at all his friends, and then said: "and all the birds that chirp and sing all day long will have a grand feast on all the caterpillars who have managed to survive the songbird's efforts to root them out and feast upon them."

"That is a good plan," Owl said kindly. "Working both day and night will surely do the job."

"That's what we think. The council worked it out."

"Let me know if you need help. Serpents hunt throughout the night, as you know. With the work going on they will be drawn to your endeavors and hunting you down. We can help protect you and your young ones."

"Thank you. That would be a tremendous help."

"Anything to save this tree. Ordinarily I wouldn't be concerned. However Creator is. And His wish is our command," the Owl replied and then blinked a few times.

"Well said. I agree. We must all work together for the good," Beaver said," turning to the others and nodding his head up and down.

"And we shall," Elly said confidently. "And we should always work together from this day forward; not only to save this tree but to save our homes and our families."

There was a solemn moment of reverence. They all quietly shook their heads approvingly in agreement just as the songbirds stopped singing and chirping. Suddenly there was a loud drumming of wings as the birds quickly flew off toward the center of the virgin forest where there was more underbrush and density. An eerie silence filled the wooded glen and all of the creatures exchanged glances in wonderment.

"What made them leave so quickly?" Elly asked, turning to The Wise-One.

Owl exchanged glances with the two Otters and with Beaver. She could sense they were just too nervous for the truth. "I'm not sure," she said, turning her attention back to the trees. "Perhaps the approaching storm from the south made them leave?" All the curious creatures glanced over the top of the young sapling and no-ticed the streaks of lighting in the far distance.

This seemed to relax them but The Wise-One knew that wasn't the only reason the songbirds quickly left the area. Creator must have warned them about the approaching Ravens and Crows that were coming from all over. They were big and black and intelligent birds that took advantage of their size and number, chasing the smaller birds away from feeding grounds to leave barely enough behind for the smaller birds. They had a habit of flying into their territory and taking it over in groups of twos and fours, or in larger flocks, an omnivorous bird with strong talons and powerful, slightly hooked beaks. Falcons were much more civil and trustworthy than the ravens. They were too war like, so that the wise old Owls and other variety of birds found it difficult to trust them, let alone be friends with too.

"I'm sure you must know," The Wise-One said to change the subject. "That those old oaks are jealous of Creator's latest creation."

"Jealous of what," Beaver asked? He licked his buckteeth, yellowed and chipped from all his days of long, hard work.

The wise Owl replied after a brief pause. "I have been told that this young sapling was created for numerous reasons, foremost to provide edible nuts to all the creatures that live nearby. It is related to the birch, those near the stream with their smooth outer barks. They can not provide tasty morsels for the birds and other creatures that dwell near this peaceful glen: the chipmunks, the squirrels, and the bears." The Owl grinned as the four-legged animals studied the young tree. "This tree will also have a gift for the creatures that walk on two legs."

"What creatures are you talking about?" Elly asked.

"And what sort of gift," Tanu asked, before Owl could respond to his mate's question?

"According to other members of my clan, including the Hawks and the Screech Owls and the Great Horned ones, they call themselves Humans. And the Albatross, who can fly across the large bodies of waters, call them animal bipes implume, two-legged animals without fur or feathers."

"If they don't have fur or feathers, how do they protect themselves?" Elly asked.

"I have yet to see these two-legged creatures. But Albatross says they have nothing to help protect them from the cold and the wind. Nor do they have any protection from the hot sun. So they make things out of wood and mud and grass. They also use the furs of animals to keep themselves warm and dry during the days of rain, and during the cold seasons when the winds are harsh and the days are snowy."

"You mean they kill our friends and relatives to survive," Tanu asked? His countenance turned fierce; he was ready to fight.

"That is what I have heard," The Wise-One replied. "I have been waiting to hear more about them. My sister will have some more news?"

"Then what is the gift that this tree is supposed to give these two-legged animals?" Tanu asked, his face still hard and bitter.

"The gift will not be for all of them. But

for some that eat the fruit of this tree will be blessed with a newborn that shall have hazel eyes; eyes that will reflect the beauty of nature throughout every single day of all the four seasons."

"But how can such a thing like that happen?" Elly wondered aloud."

"I wonder about that as well," Tanu said with a shrug.

"But isn't that what we do," Beaver asked? "Reflect the beautiful gifts that Creator gave us?"

"We do." Owl answered, blinking her large all inquiring eyes.

"So why do we need these creatures with no fur or feathers to reflect the ways of Creator?" Tanu asked severely. "It seems the gift should be one that shows them to be less callous toward our friends who live among the trees and the grasses and flowers?"

"I agree," Owl replied. "That would be nice."

"What else do these so-called humans do?" Elly asked.

"Their purpose in life is unknown to me," The Wise-One said. "But I have heard they are a troubled lot—that is, according to the messages that the Albatross and other seabirds have brought to our shores, they are not happy creatures. However, Creator gave them free will and love."

"Love," Beaver said with disgust and then grunted. "You have talked of love before."

"It is a gift that Creator gave to us centuries ago. The innate emotions that will help them feel free and good about themselves."

"How can they feel good about themselves when they kill our friends and relatives? I don't understand," Tanu said.

"I am disturbed and wonder about them too," Owl said with a hint of gloom. "But I will try to gain all the wisdom I can about them to help us. I did hear that Creator gave them emotions to help them to have compassion and a sense of meaning to their lives. They do not understand the gift as we do. We know that love is the source of life that begins in the womb. That's what makes us want to go on and survive. It is sad that these new creatures do not understand the precious gift as we understand it. They seem to be at odds with each other. And they are always searching for something they can't find. They lay their paws on rocks and blow colors of wet dust over them to make a likeness of their paw print. Only I don't think they call their paws, paws."

"Do they do that so they'll know what their

paws look like? Maybe it means something else. Maybe they put their prints on the rocks so when they leave, the other critters that pass by will think they are still there and not stick around. Maybe it means they don't like who they are?" Elly asked.

"I don't know what they think," Owl said with a hint of sadness.

"Where do they get that idea from," Tanu asked?

"It is complex," The Wise-One replied. "But hopefully the gifts that Creator has shared with them will help them. And hopefully they will soon discover that everything they do is meaningless without love. And that their eyes are the key."

"Their eyes," Beaver cut in abruptly. "There must be a purpose for these new creatures? I just don't see what their eyes have to do with anything?"

"What's wrong with our eyes?" Elly asked, after exchanging glances with her mate.

"Nothing. Not a thing," The Wise-One replied. "They are enchanting and lovely as the wild spring roses."

Elly blushed, and asked: "Then why can't these so called humans have the same color of eyes?"

"Creator sent us a message on the waves of

Gentle Breeze," The Wise-One replied. "A message I did not hear but my sister heard it quite clearly and she passed it on to me before she flew out west. It was a message that said there were all sorts of eye colors for the humans. Blue eyes that reflect the pure light of the day; green to mirror the new growth that comes every spring; brown to reflect the days of au-tumn; and black eyes to illustrate the wonders of the night. All eyes will be blessed but the ones who shall be born with Hazel eyes will be the ones that shall have the ability to reflect the true meaning of life itself, more than the others, as they shall be more understanding and connected to nature. Their eyes shall change colors with the moods of nature and also reflect the spirit of their soul and hopefully bring them closer to the wisdom that Creator wants them to have. And that is where freewill comes into play. Creator has blessed them with freedom of choice. But they, according to the message, have not truly come to understand the gift. There are rules and regulations that require diligent obedience—that is, if they want to live a happy fulfilling life. They often seek to destroy what they do not understand—and they often have wars, wars that destroy and kill. Hopefully that will end soon and they will all choose to love."

"The humans with hazel eyes," Tanu asked, somewhat confused?

"No," Owl replied, and then hooted. "All of the humans will have a choice to love. But the ones who will have eyes with earthly tones will be more inclined to embrace the ways of nature."

"Love," Beaver said gruffly. "Why do you always bring that up?" It's so embarrassing."

"I'm sorry you did not un-derstand all that I just said." Owl replied.

"I understood everything!" Beaver said defensively.

"Good. Then you know that love is everything you do to keep you strong and inclined to survive. And love, through unity, is the source of life that begins within the womb." Owl glanced over at Elly and smiled.

Elly returned the smile and blushed, holding her tummy. "How did you know?"

"You have that wonderful glow, that luminous radiance, about you," Owl replied. "And soon the life you bring into this world shall know and under-stand the beauty of your soul and the light of compassion that illuminates from your eyes and your warm smile."

"Thank you for those kind words," Elly

said softly. "But will these humans have the same qualities?"

"When they know and understand the ways of love," The Wise-One said, and then sighed deeply. "At least that is what I am hoping.and what Creator, created them for".

"I know you have spent many hours up on your lofty perch to listen to the Gentle Breeze and all of Creator's knowledge and wisdom that he sends to us," Tanu said, somewhat impatiently. "But I would like a straight answer, one that makes sense to all of us."

"And what is that?" Owl asked, obligingly.

"What will this tree have to do with the human's eyes?"

"It is all in the hands of Creator," Owl replied in her authoritative demeanor. "But, from what my cousin Spotted Owl has told me, colors must begin somewhere. And the color Hazel will begin here with this young sapling, along with all its relatives, the Hazelnut bushes and all the other young saplings."

Tanu leaned in its direction and studied the young tree for a brief moment, then asked: "So, what you have told us, these humans will somehow acquire eyes of Hazel nuts to reflect the beauty of nature and of Creator?"

"That is what I have heard; however, on one point, being that they will not have nuts for eyes, but the color of Hazel which encompasses all shades of nature. And two, the gift of seeing and understanding the beauty of wisdom—through all the things in nature. That will, hopefully, bring peace and knowledge to these troubled creatures—that is what I understand."

"I'm not so sure I do," Beaver said scratching his head.

"That is Creator's plan," Owl said assuredly. "We should never question His ways. The things of nature aren't divine in and of itself, but it displays the glory and sacredness of the Creator of all things—when that which is created reflects on the Creator. The same is imbued by the Creator to live a good life—not to themselves, but to all things created."

"It all sounds like a waste of time," Tanu said.

"You surprise me," Owl said after an amazed sigh. "You have such an intuitive soul and a heart filled with hope and confidence. You should know all there is to know about love. Soon you shall be a proud parent. And you have so much to be grateful for. The time that you and Elly have been together, the two of you do a lot of things together. You do these things out of respect and admiration for each other. Is that not correct?"

"That's true. I do get up before her and bring home the fish to eat. We do go foraging for the berries and nuts. And we do have fun playing together."

"And we mutually like those peaceful evenings," Elly added.

"That's love!" The Wise-One said.

"And we enjoy laying there in the opening of our den, watching those bright lights you call stars."

"That's love." The Owl said again with a delighted sense of superiority in her tone. She blinked away a few happy tears from her large, compassionate eyes at the Otters, then added: "Caring is also an act of love. And so is communication."

"Is that why we dug those four holes around this sickly tree?" Beaver asked.

"Yes. You came because you cared about this tree. And you did so without expecting anything in return. That is also an act of love, which is a gift from Creator, a gift that He gave to us when He created us."

"So what do we do for this tree now," Elly asked? "Why the holes?"

Before The Wise-One could respond,

streaks of lighting lit up the darkened skies to the south-west and seconds later thunder rolled across the tops of the trees near the glen and the wide open meadow.

Beaver sniffed at the refreshing scent of the advancing storm. "A heavy rain is drawing near," He said, somewhat concerned. "Maybe we should cover the holes back up? The water from the sky will surely be too much for this."

"No," Owl cut in sharply. "We must wait for the gift that must be made to save the Hazelwood."

"What sort of gift?" Tanu asked, exchanging glances with Elly and Beaver.

"A gift that shall be given freely and out of love," Owl replied.

"Does your insight tell you who will be bringing this gift?" Elly asked, somewhat suspiciously.

"Ravens," Owl replied, with a little trepidation in her tone. "And their cousins, The Crows are also flying here now."

"Why?" Elly asked fearfully.

"It don't sound good to me," Beaver piped in. "You can't trust a Raven or a Crow. They don't do anything good; they just take and take and laugh when they leave."

"Beavers' right," Tanu said. "I don't know why or what gift they have, but—"

"Creator has asked them to come," The Wise Owl said firmly. "Just as you have followed His directions so will the Ravens and the Crows. Creator shall protect us."

"So what is this special gift of theirs," Beaver asked skeptically.

"Four recently deceased couples. They are being carried here now by their brothers and sisters."

"Ravens?" Elly asked nervously. "Those big black carrion eaters are coming to our meadow' flocks and flocks of them?"

"Don't be afraid," The Wise-One said calmly again. "They will be coming to help this tree. They will not harm us. Gentle Breeze told me while I was flying overhead and observing the tree and the three of you working."

"Ravens can not be trusted," Beaver said sternly, with a hint of fear in his voice. Gift or no gift, I don't like it!"

"Ravens are known for bringing balance back to nature. And they love to create change and they have a strong sense of justice and fairness much of the time. This time they will do the right thing and lay their departed loved ones to rest near the base of this young sapling. And Creator will be pleased."

"Where there is a burial of a seed new life

springs forth." Tanu said somberly.

"That is so profoundly true," Owl agreed with a nod. "You—"

She was interrupted by the sound of loud caws and hundreds of flapping wings. The four creatures looked upward and observed an eerie sight. Black Ravens, with a bluish hue surrounding them and their cousins the Crows, were flying in from all directions. And the closer they drew near the young sapling, the darker the sky became. It was an awesome sight, as they had never seen so many groups of Ravens and Crows at any one time before. A sense of dread spread quickly through them. But it was The Wise-One who calmed their anxieties, as well as her own.

"Don't fear," she cried above the din. "Creator brought us all together to help the young Hazelwood. No harm shall come to us. Creator is in control no matter what."

"Right now I find that a little hard to believe," Elly said, her voice trembling. "But if you say Creator has brought us together to save this tree, then our fears are not justified."

Just beyond the mass of the approaching Ravens, they could smell the rain from the advancing storm. They could not see the ribbons of rain but they all knew the rain was falling from the mass of charcoal colored clouds moving toward them. It was a slow moving storm and Owl calculated that it would be upon them within the next few hours.

The Ravens and Crows arrived, turning the area around the small sapling almost completely dark with their satiny black feathers and their bluish sheen. The leader who was the largest avian of the flock, came up from the south and circled above the tree while the other members of the Crow families—landed effortlessly side-by-side on the limbs of the surrounding trees. From their point of view on the ground the four friends: the Otters, Beaver, and the wise Owl could see nothing but Ravens and Crows sitting on every branch and ever limb of the trees that surrounded the young sapling; hundreds upon hundreds of them that cast an eerie darkness. The four friends shuddered in fear but remained still.

"Now I know why all the songbirds went into hiding," Tanu whispered to Elly. "The Ravens and Crows would surely have a feast if they would have stayed."

"I just hope they don't decide to attack us," Elly whispered back, her voice trembling. She was in awe of the birds and could not take her eyes off of them, as there were so many. And in return, the Ravens and Crows were watching them with an ominous look in their militaristic dark mysterious eyes.

"Just stay calm," Tanu whispered. "Creator won't let anything like that happen. We are working together today. Just keep that in mind. Again remember Creator is in control."

Elly did not respond. She merely shook her silky head up and down, as she folded her arms across her tummy as if to protect the little one within.

A loud clamor of caws, upon caws, upon caws, by the thousands, soon filled the air and as the large black birds began chattering among them. Tanu and Elly covered their ears with their silky front paws. Beaver soon covered his own ears to drown out the mighty clamor also. But it wasn't necessary. The caws stopped with the arrival of the recently departed Ravens.

Eight Ravens, carrying a lost loved one, glided slowly around the tree and then carefully lay to rest their departed relative. A couple from each compass point was lowered side-by-side in one of the freshly dug holes. The grieving relatives, one-by-one, kicked some dirt on the dead birds and then, simultaneously, cawed out a loud, mournful song. When they were finished, they spread their dark wings and joined the other Raven's in the towering trees.

The leader of the black carrion eaters dropped down in front of The Wise-One and the others. "Within a day we shall forget our family members who have been laid to rest," he said, folding his large wings. "It is our way."

"I am sorry to hear this," Owl said with compassion.

"Thank you. But there is no need for sorrow. We choose a mate for life and it is only proper that we share our loved ones, so this new sapling will thrive."

"Creator is pleased." Owl said sincerely.

"And we are pleased to help Creator," the large Raven said, whose name was Noir ET Blu, (meaning, black and blue.) He hopped closer to Owl. "But tell me, why has He picked such a tree to give balance to this lovely land?"

Owl was cautious with his reply and said, "I have found out just a little. Soon there will be a lot of change coming to our world. This Hazelwood is supposed to be a gift to all that come to know it for its beauty, its fruit, and its healing leaves."

"Can it be saved by what we have done?" Noir ET Blu, the Raven asked.

"Only time and Creator can know," The Wise-One replied, blinking her large eyes. "But my intuition is telling me that it will be saved, thanks in part to the gift you and your fellow Raven's have brought here today."

"Very good, Raven said. He paused to search the eyes of Beaver and then the eyes of the two Otters. "I sense and I see their apprehension," he said, leering deep into Owl's eyes. "Why do you fear us?" He asked, toying with his words.

"It may seem that way," Owl replied. "It's just that we have never seen so many of you at one time. And you must admit it's a great show of force as well as an awesome sight."

"Gracious lady, we mean you no harm."

"We thank you. It is well said! But it is your numbers more than anything that is impressive." Owl wasn't about to show any lack of courage, or any fear for that matter. "To see members of the Crows and Ravens together is a glorious sight. Our Creator has indeed blessed both of your species. Your numbers are impressive."

"If numbers frighten you, wait until you see the new creatures; the animals with no fur nor feathers; the wicked ones with dark and mysterious ways. They are big and they come by the thousands."

"You have seen these creatures?" Owl asked.

"They are coming down from the northwest with different ways of communicating," Raven went on, ignoring Owl's question. "And they have settled alongside the rivers that flow into the large body of water that no one can drink. And they have begun to move inland and they dwell down in the land of sand and hot rocks. Some are even moving over the mountains to the west."

"Then it's true," Beaver said with a hint of fear in his voice, "they are coming our way?"

"That is what I hear," Raven replied.

"But have you seen them?" The Wise-One asked again.

"Not yet. But my fellow Ravens and our cousins the Crows from the west have seen them. And so have the coastal birds. In fact, some of the seagulls that encountered them have moved inland to escape their brutality. They want nothing to do with these two-legged creatures. They destroy everything without regard to the feelings of others. They are a wicked lot, these creatures. And why Creator has allowed them to do what they do is beyond us and our brothers and sisters."

"What did the seagulls have to say about

them?"

"I have yet to speak with a gull, but my cousin from the west has told me many things. They fight among themselves, often to the death. And they cut down trees to build shelters, and make great flames that get out of control and destroy much land and animals. They use strange looking objects to hunt and kill the fish and other animals of nature. It appears they fear all the animals of the woods. Yet they go into the deep forests and high mountains to hunt them down for food and other things. They aren't satisfied with the same fruits and grasses that the much bigger animals eat." Raven paused to look around. He had everyone's attention and this pleased him. "They do other wicked things to the creatures that dwell wherever they show up. They go on large hunting parties and kill rabbits by the hundreds. And they kill our kind as well, especially the wild turkeys. They also hunt and kill the Eagles, the Hawks, the Crows and my brothers and sisters—and your relatives, too. And then they just leave them there to rot."

"And what about us," Beaver asked nervously?

"I have heard they kill your kind to keep warm when the cold wind from the north comes and when the rain turns to snow. They also hunt the sea otters for their furs," Raven said, looking at Elly and Tanu.

The two Otters hugged each other and Elly began to cry. Tanu wiped the tears from her eyes.

"I was afraid something like this would happen when I first heard about these odd looking creatures," The Wise-One said, after wiping a tear from her huge right eye. "My instincts were right. These creatures are a part of the change that comes. But it seems the changes that they will bring to our land will not be in our best interest."

"That is what Coyote thinks too," Raven said with a hint of sadness. "I have heard the tricksters wailing during the nights where I dwell. When I spoke with one, he told me the humans don't take the time to speak with them. They kill them and then stretch their fur to be dried by the orb that gives us light." Raven paused to see if all were still listening. Again he was pleased to see he had a captive audience. He continued: "That is what our cousins the crows have told us, too. And that concerns us deeply."

"It concerns us all," Owl said. "Perhaps this new sapling will help?"

"I don't see how? But that is our hope as

well," Noir ET Blu said, nodding his head in agreement. "But as you have said, only time will tell. If Creator has designed this plan that must come to our land, it must eventually work. Time is seen differently for us than it is by the Creator. Who are we to question Creator?"

"Yes, time will tell!" The Wise-One said, blinking her eyes again.

"I suggest that you go into hiding when they begin to enter your territory. Don't let them see you."

"Is that what you and your fellow Ravens are going to do?"

"That is precisely what we intend to do. We are not fools. Some of us have been killed for our feathers alone. For ceremonial garments as they call their clothes. Some of the creatures make ridiculous ornaments to wear on their heads and drape long capes behind their shoulders made of thousands of bird feathers. They think it is beautiful and some think that powerful leaders of their tribes should wear them as symbols of their greatness. Can you believe that?"

"I believe it," Beaver said with a hint of fear in his tone. "And when they come to our land I shall go into hiding, just as you said you will do."

"So are we," Tanu said with resolve. We'll do what we have to do—for our survival. We will miss the freedom to roam far and wide without a care or worry. Frolicking, through the seasons, playing with all the other creatures we meet along the way. I will miss the stories never to be heard again because humans are coming our way."

"I know you are not fools," Raven replied. "And that is good. They do not smell good and you will know they are coming by their hideous smell. I have yet to smell them but my cousins tell me that it is like no other smell that you have encountered. And when you smell them, you must go into hiding as quickly as you can, for they shall be on the hunt."

"You mean they will be coming to destroy us?" Beaver said with trembling.

"Yes," Raven said evenly and with a sinister tone in his voice. "We had a large council meeting weeks ago and decided to attack them. But Creator spoke to us through the breeze that moves the leaves. He said it would not be wise. He said to just let the humans be and to just go into hiding whenever they approach. And He said to tell all the birds and the other creatures to do the same."

"Then we shall do as you have said," The Wise-One replied. Did Creator say anything else?"

Noir ET Blu, the large Raven shook his head from side-to-side, said goodbye and then hopped over to the nearest grave and kicked dirt into the hole. The other large birds, in-groups of twos and fours, flew down from their lofty perches and kicked dirt into the graves. It took a good hour for the birds to bury their loved ones. And when it was done, they filled the air with their loud and mournful caws and then flew off in the directions from which they came, saying nothing more to the Owl, Beaver, or to the Otters.

Minutes later, the Otters and Beaver walked to the graves and patted the loose earth down so that the approaching wind and rain would not blow or wash the new turned earthly graves away. The Owl spread its wings and flew over the tree, circling and trying her best to sing a mournful song. But it only sounded like a repetitive call of Who, who, who, compared to the Ravens thunderous caws. When she was finished, The Wise-One flew off into the woods without so much as saying a word of farewell to her friends.

Finished with their work, the water loving creatures nodded their heads at each other in silence and then went their separate ways. The

Otters, in their concern for the Hazelwood, turned around and sniffed the air. Except for the smell of freshly dug earth nothing had changed. The smell of summer was in the air and the approaching storm from the south was bringing the smell of new life with it. The two Otters could make out all the different fragrances and this excited them. The plan was to find a few filbert saplings that could be cross pollinators, for the one they just finished helping. They became playful and joyful, knowing that the promise of renewal was approaching. The young sapling would live, their intuitions told them that, and soon they would know more and understand the reasons as to why Creator had made such a beautiful tree.

The Wise-One, perched high near the opening of her nest, sat quietly and watched Elly and Tanu and Beaver leave the young sapling. She glanced around her by flicking her head quickly whenever she saw movement near the tree. She knew the smell of the freshly dug earth would eventually bring some of the other creatures to the tree, and she was hoping for a nice big field mouse to fill her empty stomach. But the first to arrive was the skittish rabbit. She would have flown down to capture it but she noticed it had young ones with her, so The Wise-One decided to leave them alone—that is, if they left the tree alone. Besides, she told herself, too much rabbit in one week isn't good for the digestive system.

The rabbits proved to be no threat to the young sapling. They sniffed at the fresh dirt and quickly left the area, moving up through the open meadow to their underground den. A good twenty minutes later, The Wise-One had her meal. A large, fat field mouse, drawn out of its den with curiosity, darted out of the tall grass and sniffed at the graves. The Wise-One captured it quickly and just before the first gust of wind and large raindrops hit the edge of the virgin forest, she had consumed the mouse, flew down to the stream to wash and to drink her fill, and then flew back up to her lofty perch.

With the first few raindrops, The Wise-One crawled inside her den and prepared herself for a long, wet afternoon and evening. She placed large sticks in front of her den opening, then some leaves and straw to help ward off the wetness. When she was finished, The Wise-One moved to the far corner and tucked her head under her wing and fell asleep.

The wind was the first to arrive. It blew hard and steady, shaking the trees back and forth while the rain fell hard and the bolts of lightning lit up the virgin forest. All the creatures that lived in the forest were thankful for the rain and thankful that the bolts of lightning were streaking across the sky and not coming down to destroy someone's home.

The storm lasted throughout the afternoon and into the night. It finally moved off toward the northeast a good three hours before the sun began to rise in the eastern sky.

The Wise-One was wide-awake before the storm had departed. When the winds died down and the rain stopped, she removed her straw and sticks and emerged from her den. She spread her wings, stretching them as far as she could, and then flew down to chat with the young sapling.

"Good morning, young Hazelwood," she said after landing near the young tree. "I see you're looking much better." The Wise-One waddled around the tree and stopped near the lowest hanging branch. She examined it closely. "You are so lucky, you know? Those caterpillars have not noticed you and hopefully they won't before the Beavers can chew down those sickly oak trees. And then allow the songbirds to feast on the pests that have destroyed your distant relatives. But I know you are grateful for our efforts to protect you. I also know that Creator has spoken with you and assured you that all of us will protect you. Yesterday was a bad day for you, and you were so depressed. But I have heard the thanks when Gentle Breeze caresses your leaves. And the others, who will help you in the days, weeks, and months and years ahead, will know you are grateful. And it is a wondrous sight to see that you are beginning to share your flowers and your fruit." The Wise-One stood silent and listened to the young tree's leaves. "You have nothing to worry about," she said after the leaves stopped shimmering. "We will kill the caterpillars and any insects that linger on your leaves and your strong bark—that is, if it is necessary after Beaver and his relatives destroy the dying trees. I have spoken with the songbirds and they will visit you each day and examine you thoroughly. That is our promise to both you and to Creator. You will survive."

The Wise-One listened to the young tree's leaves again, then thanked the tree for thanking her, and then flew back up to her lofty perch. There she kept a close watch around the young sapling and the nearby stream, hoping a snake would soon show itself. Nothing like a delicious snake for breakfast, she told herself.

A few minutes later she turned and watched her sister, Gog, as she flew in from the west and landed next to The Wise-One's perch. They greeted each other with kind and loving words and hugs. Gog was the first to speak after the heartfelt greetings they gave to each other.

"I have seen the creatures without furs or feathers," she said, blinking her large eyes to stop her tears. "They are a strange breed."

"So I have heard," The Wise-One said. "The Raven's were here yesterday and they say these so-called creatures are wicked. And that they kill our kind just for the sport of it. And leave our fellow birds to just rot in the sun."

"You cannot believe the words of those Raven's," Gog said. "Yes, they do hunt to survive and they only take what they need. Just as you and I hunt to survive, so do these humans."

"I should have known the Raven was over exaggerating."

"He was and I know why. They were upset because Creator had made them promise to leave you and your friends alone. They had come from a long distance and they were hungry. They wanted to attack and devour you and your friends."

"Who told you this?" The Wise-One asked, after swallowing the lump of fear in her throat.

"It was late and the rain was falling so I took shelter in the den of an old squirrel's home in a large thick spruce that had been killed by lightning years ago. And just below me, Ravens took shelter in a den at the base of the tree. I overheard them talking about you and your friends and the young sapling and how easy it would have been to kill and eat you and your friends."

"I should have known. I almost let my guard down." The Wise-One shuddered and felt a chill. "I must thank Creator for watching out for us."

"The creatures without feathers call Creator by another name. They say He is the Great Spirit."

"The Great Spirit," Owl asked, looking somewhat bewildered?

"Yes, and they claim that everything that dwells upon this land is a gift from the Great Spirit. And that everything has its own spirit, which they call Inues. Even the air has one. And the human Inue is the soul."

"The humans have a soul? Like us?"

"An Inue," Gog replied.

"What did they say about us?"

"The creatures did not talk about us. But I did hear them say that everything that the Great Spirit put on H'Uraru, the Earth, must be respected."

"The Earth?"

"Yes. And the Great Spirit's home is in a place they call Olelpanti."

"What does that mean?"

"It bothered me for days. And then one night, during the first full moon of the warm season, a mother sat with her sons on a large rock above my perch. They spoke of Olelpanti as a sacred place, where sacred spirits dwell after they have left this place."

"You could understand them," Owl asked?

"The Creator had the leaves interpret their meaning. The woman with children spoke with her tongue and with her hands and body, moving all around, up and down, and sideways. It was a strange experience to watch and to learn."

The Wise-One studied her sister's face and then gazed around her, taking in the beauty of the virgin forest in with a deep and respectful sigh of deep pleasure.

"Perhaps Creator wants us to know of these things? Perhaps that is why she sent you west to observe these creatures with no feathers?"

"I thought about that during my journey home," Gog said, "and I do believe you are right. We must come to terms with these new creatures. It will be in our best interest to understand them and their ways."

"I agree," The Wise-One said slowly. "It does make sense."

"One of the things that I have already learned is that they do not like the black Crows or the Ravens. Some have spoken of the Raven as a trickster, an evil bird they call Wigit!"

"Wigit?"

"A bird that cannot be trusted."

"I can understand that."

They were interrupted by the sound of a flock of chickadees. They landed on a short sandbar alongside the stream and then quickly darted into and under the scraggly and thorny bushes that lined the banks of the stream. Moments later they both understood why the small birds went into hiding. A brown bear sow with her two cubs came into view, slowly taking their time as they moved downstream.

"Is that Ursu?" Gog asked, after a brief silence.

"Looks like her," The Wise-One replied, as she studied the large omnivores. "She must be searching for wild berries this morning."

The two Owls watched the three bears in silence. When they had passed peacefully and disappeared on the other side of the stream, the two inquisitive and wise Owls continued with their discussion.

"What else did you learn? The Ravens told us yesterday that these creatures with no feathers and no fur are wicked and destroy everything in their path—and that they smell bad!"

"The Ravens were overstating facts. Yes, they do smell somewhat. They smell of wood smoke. And some times they smell like the ones that they go after in their hunts."

"While you were gone I have been listening to Creator speak with the help of Gentle Breeze and the tingling of the tree leaves. Did you have a chance to listen as well?"

"Almost daily," Gog said with a nod. "He gave me some insight about the humans."

"What about their love and understanding of nature's ways? Did you hear anything about the gifts that Creator was to give them?"

"From what I understand, through both my observations and from what Creator has shared with me, most of these humans have a deep understanding of love and of Creators ways."

"Are you sure?"

"I think so. They seem to be a closely-knit society and they teach their young ones to respect all of the Great Spirit's Inues."

"What do you mean," The Wise Owl asked?

"About Inues," Gog asked?

"You mentioned that name but I have never heard of it before," Owl said.

"The new creatures, the humans, believe that everything we see has its own spirit. They call them Inues."

"Even the grass and the trees," Wise Owl asked?

Gog nodded her head up and down and said: "They fear this Great Spirit and worship him in many ways. They sing to him and they dance, and they pray to this spirit!"

"Did you see this Great Spirit?"

"No. But what I observed, the Great Spirit is everywhere at all times and knows everything."

"Just like our Creator?"

"Yes," Gog replied, slowly nodding her head.

"I am pleased with this news. Perhaps the changes that will come will be good and in our interest?"

"I hope you're right."

"What about their eyes? What color were

they?"

"They had dark eyes. Mostly brown and black."

"No green or gray or blue eyes?"

"No, I did not see those colors."

"Hummp," The Wise-One said, then asked: "What was the color of their skin?"

"Most were a light or a dark brown; some almost a reddish brown. All of them had long black hair". Gog searched The Wise-One's face. "Why do you ask these questions?"

"I was told there would be humans with all sorts of eye colors to help reflect the beauty of this place. Now I am slightly troubled and confused? I don't know what to think now?"

"Perhaps there are other kinds living elsewhere who do have the other colors of eyes that you mentioned. The Condor who flies great distances should be consulted."

"Maybe you're right?" The Wise-One said after a short pause. "Are you hungry?"

"Starving," Gog replied. "What do you see?"

"Two large serpents," The Wise-One said, nodding her head toward the stream. "Just on the other side near the large rock."

"Yes, I see them. Which one do you want?"

"I'll take the smaller of the two. You can have the big one who is now drinking from the stream."

The two large Owls swiftly and silently flew from their perch and easily captured the deadly serpents. After scooping them up they both flew high
into the sky and then dropped the snakes among the rocks alongside the stream. Then they flew down and picked up the dead serpents and flew back to their lofty perch to have a hearty breakfast.

Later that morning, Elly and Tanu lay near the young Hazelwood tree. The early morning air was filled with the freshness of sweet smelling pines, the wild roses and the purple heather and sage. The nearby lakes were warming and a thick mist was rising slowly, working its way through the trees and dissipating into the cloudless sky. The young Hazelwood was showing signs of revival, and this delighted the two Otters.

"What are you thinking?" Elly asked, snuggling closer to her mate.

Tanu turned to face Elly and placed a loving paw on her face.

"I was thinking of how I felt when I first saw you sliding down that muddy slope and into the stream."

"I remember that day," she said with a gleam in her eyes. "And how did you feel?"

"Alive."

"Really?"

"For the first time in my life I truly felt alive. And that is how this young Hazelwood must feel." He turned to face the tree. "Look at her limbs and her leaves. See how much they have changed since late yesterday. There is love within her. And that love will soon spread joy and beauty throughout this wondrous place." He turned to face Elly again. "Just like you fill my heart with wonder and beauty; I will always get lost in the love and the wisdom you hold in your eyes. And I shall always feel blessed with the beauty of your smile."

"I feel the same way about you," Elly said softly and lovingly. "Out of all the precious gifts that nature has given me, you are the flame within my heart and within my soul."

The two Otters hugged and rubbed noses and then holding each other tight, turned their attention back to the Hazelwood tree and listened to all the amazing sounds of the virgin forest as the Sun finally came up over the tall mountains to the east.

The songbirds had come out shortly after the day had started and their throaty melodies filled the forest and the meadow with a symphony of love songs and songs of praise to Creator. A few of the bright colored birds flew down and landed on the young sapling. Elly and Tanu watched in silence as the birds fluttered from limb to limb, checking both the top and the bottom of the tree's leaves. When the two birds were satisfied that the young tree was not infected with caterpillars, they flew back up into the thick trees.

And with the breaking of the new day, a few honeybees arrived and began to work on both the male and the female flowers. And shortly thereafter the sound of gnawing filled the air. The Otters stood up on their hind legs and smiled. Beaver and his relatives were just beginning to tackle the sickly birch and oak trees. And directly above them, The Wise-One and her relatives were standing guard, as promised, to protect them from the serpents that lived nearby under old fallen trees and in old homes that once belonged to the field mice.

"How long do you suppose it will take them?" Elly asked.

"Beaver will keep his word. Two, maybe three days," Tanu replied with a shrug. "They will keep at it until the task is complete." The cross pollinators have been located. They are just beyond the willows where the water bends."

"And how many seasons will it take for this young Hazel to begin spreading its beauty across the land?"

"From the looks of things I do believe the process has already begun."

The two Otters smiled at each other and after a short pause, Elly asked: "Were you surprised that Owl knew of my condition?"

"No. She is a wise one. And you do radiate such a lovely glow. You are beautiful, you know?" Elly blushed and snuggled closer. "I can't wait to see our first pup," Tanu said proudly. "I just know it will have your eyes and your gentle spirit."

"Have you thought of any names?" Elly asked, searching her mate's eyes.

"I like the name you have picked for the female, Phoebe."

"And what have you decided for your son?"

"I like Tanu."

"But that's your name. We can't have two Tanus running around."

"Well, maybe you're right," Tanu said with a sheepish grin. "What about Tule?"

"Tule," Elly asked with a disgusted look? "The reeds that grow in the water; you must be kidding?"

Tanu laughed. Elly playfully nudged him in

the side.

"Okay, that's enough," Tanu said smiling.

"Then give me a name!" Elly demanded with a smile that brightened Tanu's heart. "You must decide today."

"Is it about time?" Tanu asked, turning serious.

"It is. Maybe by tomorrow."

Tanu held Elli's lovely and mysterious eyes in his and he fell in love with her all over again. And not wanting this affectionate moment to end, his playful nature took over and he fell to his side. Elly reached out to catch him and asked: "What are you doing?" She asked playfully.

"I'm falling in love again. Don't catch me."

Elly smiled and laughed, and then said: "You silly doodle! We must be serious. What about a name for our newborn? You must decide, and soon."

"Let's stick with Tanu," He whispered softly. "Okay?"

"Are you sure?" Elly asked, nudging his nose with hers.

"Yes. I like that name and would be proud to give it to my son."

"Okay," Elly said warmly, "you can call your son Tanu."

They rubbed noses and hugged and then

stood on their hind legs and studied the tree. A beam of early morning sunlight fell upon the tree through the fad-ing mist and the tall trees. They both marveled at the tree's beauty under the brief few minutes that the sunlight fell upon the young sapling.

"The Wise-One was right," Elly said. "This young tree does need more sunlight."

"Yes, it does," Tanu said. "And it will, thanks to Beaver and his relatives and friends. And when this tree reaches its fullest potential, our children's children will come to know and respect it just as we have. I just hope the so-called humans will come to know it as we have come to know it."

"They will. Where there is love there is hope."

"Who told you that?"

"Gentle Breeze gave me that feeling; that sense of hope, just today, when she slipped into our den and caressed my face to awaken me."

"That same breeze awoke me and I felt a sense of brightness."

"And do you still feel this hopefulness?"

"I do," Tanu replied, taking Elli's furry paw in his, "more than ever. The future for our young ones and for this tree and for all the other creatures who walk and fly over this wonderful land will be filled with enthusiasm and understanding. Nature shall provide a sense of harmony for all."

"I hope you are right, my love. I hope you are right." Elly grabbed her stomach and moaned. "It is time. Let us go back to our den."

Tanu took Elly in his strong arms and helped her back to their den. The Gentle Breeze picked up to carry the news that a newborn Otter would soon be playing in the Virgin forest.

The Wise-One, upon hearing the news through the tingling leaves, left her perch while her sister continued to watch over the beavers. The Wise-One arrived just as Tanu was helping Elly into the den.

"What is it?" Tanu asked.

"I have come to assist you," The Wise-One said, her eyes filled with tears of joy. "To protect your den from the serpents and other creatures who would love to devour a newborn pup."

"Thank you," Tanu said. "You are a dear friend."

"You just take care of your mate and the joy she will soon deliver to you. I will watch the front of your den and protect you."

"Thank you again," Tanu said and quickly

slipped into his den. Moments later, he stuck his head out. "And when you get the chance, thank Creator for us. He is truly the good one."

"Creator is everywhere and He knows how you feel," The Wise-One said. "He is a spirit that is all knowing and all caring, and no matter where you are, He is with you and knows your thoughts and the feelings of your heart. We may not always understand His ways and why He does what He does, but He knows you and He protects you. And that is something we can always count on."

Tanu thanked The Wise-One again and then went back inside to tend to Elly. Owl flew up and perched herself on the strong limb of a large pine that overlooked the den of the two Otters.

Within the hour Elly gave birth to a sweet and healthy daughter they called Phoebe, which means bright and shining. When he was certain that Elly and his daughter were okay, he scurried out of his den and told The Wise-One and the other Otters who had dropped by to pay their respects. News of the newborn Otter spread quickly throughout the virgin forest. And by the time the full moon was hanging high above the Otter's den, many of their friends had stopped by with their respects and to bring nuts and berries and a few fish for all to enjoy.

And during the festive occasion, The Wise-One's sister joined her and the two remained perched on the lofty pine to protect everyone from the deadly serpents who hunt at night. And for both of them it was a good night. Three times they flew down and snatched up large rattlers and shared the meat with their fellow sisters and brothers, who had faithfully lingered over the Beavers who had worked almost nonstop to bringing down the old, caterpillar infested Oaks and birches.

And it was just before daybreak that the trees started coming down, falling away from the young Hazel wood to land near and across the stream. And just as the sun began to cast its light over the virgin forest, the songbirds, hundreds of them, came out of the trees and started to feast on the caterpillars and other insects that had been killing the two large Oaks and birches. And while they feasted, Beaver and his relatives wobbled off to the lake and dove in to cool off and wash up. Tanu came over to the part of the stream where they were washing.

"Have you heard the news?" Tanu asked.

"About your daughter," Beaver asked? "Yes, I have. Congratulations."

"Thank you. But The Wise-One's older sister Gog has returned and says the Ravens were overstating the facts about the humans."

"I'll wait and see for myself," Beaver said, scrubbing behind his right ear. "And if I were you, I'd stay on my guard as well."

"Well, perhaps you're right. But let's discuss it later. You and your family are welcome to come over when you have rested. We will have plenty of nuts and berries put aside for all of you."

"Thank you, my friend. We shall come for a visit."

Beaver said goodbye and dove under the water to swim home. Tanu quickly made his way back home to tend to his newborn daughter and his lovely wife, Elly. And on the way home he came up with a loving poem for her. He snatched a mouthful of lovely wild flowers and upon giving them to Elly, Tanu recited his affectionate thoughts:

My sweet and lovely Elly
I shall make a slide for you
Of the wettest and smoothest pile of
muddy goo
To teach our child how to play, for days
and days of fun
Just as you and I have had,

playing in the sun
Where you and I have always had loads and
loads of fun

Tanu knelt down and kissed the tears from her eyes.

"You are so sweet and loving," she said, reaching up to caress his face. "That was beautiful. Thank you."

Tanu took her hand and held her enchanting eyes in his. "Thank you for being in love with me. And thank you for such a beautiful daughter. That glow, that radiance you had, the one The Wise-One mentioned, is still with you. I doubt if you'll ever lose it."

"It's you. You make me glow with everything that you do. Don't ever change, okay?"

"I promise. I'll always be the way I am. And it is you that I can thank for helping me to be the way I am."

The two Otters nuzzled and then held each other tight while Phoebe nestled close in her mother's arms.

A season and three months later, Tanu and Elly brought Phoebe and their second daughter of five months, Anac, who, like her older sister, was daddy's little chatterbox and could not get enough of his love and attention, came to view the young sapling. The virgin forest was beginning to change colors and the two playful young Otters marveled at the beauty of the young tree. They sat in silence as Gentle Breeze, somewhat cooler, whispered through the leaves of the Hazelwood. It was grateful for their help and told them that they could be the first to sample its fruit. Tanu moved closer to the tree and saw three large filberts hanging down from the center limb. He reached up and picked them and brought them back to his wife and daughters. They were hard nuts to crack open, but with a lot of persistence Tanu soon had the tasty morsels evenly divided among the four of them. As they devoured the nuts the breeze picked up again and the Hazelwood began to fill the meadow with a sweet song of thanks and of gratitude and of love.

The Wise-One flew down from her lofty perch and after a little coaxing from Tanu and Elly, she tasted the morsels. The wise Owl was pleased with the taste and thanked the Otters for sharing their meal.

"What about your sister?" Tanu asked. "Do you want to give her some?"

"She's not living with me now," The Wise-One said with a smile. "She moved in with a mate and they live north of here, near the foot of the large mountains."

"What about you?" Elly asked. "Do you have a mate?"

"Not yet. But there are two who are trying to capture my eye."

"Do you have a preference?" Elly asked.

"Not yet. I am not ready to mate. Perhaps by this time next year. I am considering it carefully."

"And I am sure you will pick the right one," Tanu said.

"Thank you. I will do my best."

"I'm sure you will," Tanu said, as he handed a small piece of the fruit to his oldest daughter. Anac gave her daddy a pouting whimper and Tanu gave in, giving her another piece of his serving. Her eyes lit up and that was all the thanks Tanu needed. She had the eyes of her mother and whenever she looked up at him, his heart would just melt and his body tingled with pride.

"We should pick a few for Beaver and his family," Elly said, after licking her lips. "They should know what these nuts taste like."

"I agree," Tanu said, then moved down to the tree and gingerly removed two large filberts. He brought them back and sat them down in front of Elly. "We can give these two treats to them tomorrow."

"There are others who have been waiting for this moment," The Wise-One said. "There are chipmunks and squirrels waiting in the tall grass near the edge of the tree line. And the birds who sing night and day are waiting as well."

"Should we invite them over?" Elly asked.

"I must leave first," The Wise-One said. "And yes, that would be the sensible thing to do. Invite them all over, they'll be safe."

"But why must you leave?" Tanu asked. "Do they all fear you that much?"

"They do. But that is my concern and not yours. After I am gone, signal to them that it's okay to come and visit the young tree. And then help them crack open the nuts. They will in turn begin to spread the seeds of this new breed of tree throughout the forest." The Wise-One said goodbye and then flew off toward her den in the large spruce.

Elly and Tanu both stood on their hind legs and beckoned the others to join them. Soon both the songbirds and the other four-legged creatures surrounded the young Hazelwood tree. Tanu and Elly and the chipmunks and squirrels helped crack open the nuts and allowed the birds to feast on the tasty morsels. The Wise-One kept her eyes open for any trouble makers who might show up and easily dispatched two large rattlesnakes that had been following the sent of the chipmunks by tasting the rocks and dirt with their forked tongues. The Wise-One's actions had not gone unnoticed and all the creatures waved and thanked her, especially the two chipmunks that had always considered The Wise-One and her kind to be mortal enemies.

A few seasons later, the Hazelwood tree stood proud and tall and grateful. And with each passing season she had more and more enjoyable nuts for all the creatures who lived nearby—and for those who came from a distance to taste the fruit that the Hazelwood was happy to provide. And they all marveled at the sight of the male and female flowers that sprouted from the tree. She produced male flowers in catkins and female flowers in colorful clusters. And with each passing season, new Hazelwood trees and shrubs began to dot the landscape, spreading beauty and food to all the flocks of birds, including the red-winged black birds; the dull gray sparrows; and robins, the birds known best for bringing the first signs of spring to the virgin forest. The Hazelwood trees were also glad to see the yellow-breasted robins, and all the other finches and thrushes that came to eat its fruit and to spread its seeds across the landscape. Even the Ravens and the Crows came to feast on the filberts and to spread the seeds of the first Hazelwood.

And within the next few centuries, the Hazelwood spread throughout the entire world. Some of the saplings became nothing more than lovely shrubs while others grew to be nine feet in height, others as tall as thirty feet. And all gave life back to the creatures that had helped it to grow and spread throughout the continents.

And centuries later, when the creatures with no feathers began to dominate the land and study its ways, some of the humans that came and marveled over the beauty of the Hazelwood shrubs and trees, and consume their edible filberts, were later blessed with children with Hazel eyes. Eyes that shone like silver leaves among the evergreens; eyes that mirrored the glorious miracles that Creator gave to all the creatures that roam the gentle valleys and meadows, rolling hills, and mountains of His celestial domain.

That is how the Hazelwood came to be— and how the glorious gift of hazel eyes came into existence. Just like he gave the gift of eyes of blue, gray, brown, black, and green, to observe and reflect the wonders of The

Hazel Eyes – A Fable

Creator, to respect and see all of His creatures and their individual ways, and to fulfill His wish that all creatures shall come to know the beauty that surrounds them; to give them a sense of reverence for themselves and for others. And to allow them to love with open minds and hearts of wonder and joy, so that they will know and understand that The Creator is filled with a heart of love, empathy, mercy, grace, and wisdom that He gives to all of his living creations. He is the Rock that all creatures, large and small, need to cling to, to make their lives more peaceful and eternal. He is the source of all knowledge that He lovingly shares with the righteous who lean out for enlightenment; wisdom to cope with life's difficulties. Through others and through observations and through their findings and through their wisdom they collect daily, each one has to come to terms with the blessings and lessons of nature. And, with helping each other, they can all live within the circles of peace and trust, along with a love for the gifts that each one has to offer their neighbors to survive within a harmony that resonates from every blade of grass, every tree, every brook, and every song from the wildlife and birds, to the gleeful playful otters and beavers. As for the first Hazelwood tree, she stands firm and

Marvin L. Patton and Carol J. Gerrior-Patton

healthy within the Virgin forest where humankind has yet to see her splendor. The creatures of the forest protect her, especially the descendents of Tanu and Elly, Otters who playfully live on and eat the extraordinary fruit of the Hazelwood.

THE END